YOUNG PEOPLE'S LIBRARY SERVICE
LONGTOWN

CUMBRIA LIBRARY SERVICES

Cumbria
COUNTY COUNCIL

This book is due to be returned on or before the last date above. It may be renewed by personal application, post or telephone, if not in demand.

C.L.18

For Chris Pearson

**Find out more about the Scaredy Cats
at Shoo's fabulous website:
www.shoo-rayner.co.uk**

ORCHARD BOOKS
96 Leonard Street, London EC2A 4XD
Orchard Books Australia
32/45-51 Huntley Street, Alexandria, NSW 2015
First published in Great Britain in 2004
First paperback edition 2005
Copyright © Shoo Rayner 2004
The right of Shoo Rayner to be identified as the author
and illustrator of this work has been asserted by him in
accordance with the Copyright, Designs, and Patents Act, 1988.
A CIP catalogue record for this book is available
from the British Library.
ISBN 1 84362 440 0 (hardback)
ISBN 1 84362 729 9 (paperback)
1 3 5 7 9 10 8 6 4 2 (hardback)
1 3 5 7 9 10 8 6 4 2 (paperback)
Printed in Great Britain

Frankatstein

ORCHARD BOOKS

One evening, Fifi sneaked out of the chemist shop where she lived and froze. The silhouette of a gigantic, slavering monster loomed over her.

Fifi's fur stood up on end. She
screeched and ran.

The mad howling followed her...

At the end of the street, Fifi's friend,
Daisy, caught up with her.

Together they raced across the
nearby fields, never stopping until they
came to the secret circle.

The other seven members of the secret society of Scaredy Cats were waiting impatiently.

"I-I-I-I was attacked by a monster!" Fifi panted.

"No you w-w-weren't!" Daisy gasped. "I-I-it was me," she explained when she got her breath back. "I was waving and calling to you from my front door. You only saw my shadow!"

"But..." Fifi was lost for words.

Her friends rolled their eyes. Fifi was always getting things muddled.

"Though you never know what lurks in the shadows," growled Kipling, their leader.

Silence fell upon the secret circle.
Kipling's eyes narrowed into slits.
He was ready to tell a story. The
story they had all come to hear...

"This is a story about a brother and sister I once knew called Kendo and Suki," Kipling began. "They lived with Professor Frankatstein."

Professor Frankatstein spent every waking hour on his life's work. A crazy project to create life itself!

Kendo and Suki provided the mice and rats for the professor's experiments. The two cats were his very special assistants.

Kendo and Suki loved to watch the professor work. By poking wires into brains and flicking switches, he made dead bodies twitch as though they were alive!

One day, the incredible happened.
A small brown mouse came back to
life on the operating table.

Life was there in the mouse's dark
shining eyes.

The professor turned up the power.
The little body trembled, but then the
eyes closed and the life that was there
faded away.

The Professor whispered to his cats,
"I need a bigger body to work on."

Kendo and Suki understood. That night they hunted through the darkened alleys until they cornered an enormous grey rat.

Kendo leaped into action straight away and chased the rat, while Suki covered its escape routes.

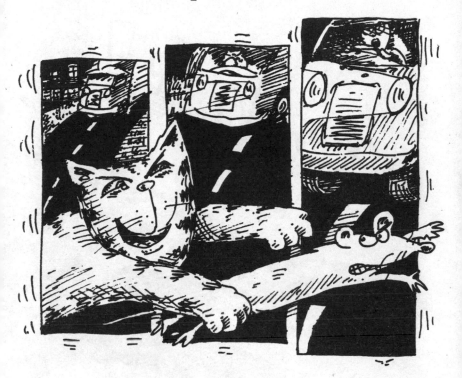

As Kendo chased the rat out into the road he had no thought for his own safety.

The truck squealed as the driver hit the brakes, but it was too late...Kendo didn't have a chance.

When Suki returned home, alone
and heartbroken, Professor Frankatstein
followed her back to find the gory
remains of her brother.

With tears in his eyes, he scraped up all the bits he could find and put them into a jar.

"I will make Kendo live again," he told Suki. "I promise I will bring your brother back to life."

Suki was desperate. She felt as though half of her had been wrenched away. The Professor worked tirelessly around the clock to save Kendo.

Bits of rat had been squished together with Kendo's body. It was hard to separate the two.

At last everything was ready, tubes
and wires were attached to Kendo's
lifeless body.

The air crackled with electricity. Lights flickered as Professor Frankatstein adjusted the controls. A strange smell of burning tinged the air.

From behind a row of test-tubes,
Suki watched the body twitch
and writhe.

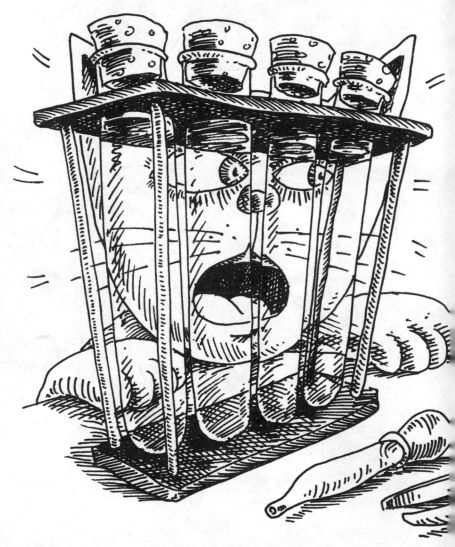

Slowly, its eyes opened. Trembling and groaning, it raised itself up and looked around, dazed and confused.

Suki's heart leaped. Kendo was alive!
He was really alive again! And
yet…there was something different
about him…something sneaky,
something…ratty!

The professor picked Kendo up.
"Welcome back, my precious Kendo,"
he soothed. "Now the world will know
what a genius I am!"

Rage flickered across Kendo's eyes...

His claws lashed out...

Professor Frankatstein howled with pain.

Kendo sprang from the professor's arms and bounded out of the laboratory in search of freedom.

As the weeks went by, stories of a strange wild animal spread through the town. Pets disappeared in the night… guinea pigs, rabbits, even small dogs.

Vicious traps were set to catch
the beast.

Night after night, the heartbroken
Suki searched for her lost brother.

Until, one night, Suki felt all her senses tingling. *She* was being hunted!

A terrifying black shape leaped out of the darkness. With a blood-curdling cry, it sank its drooling teeth into the soft flesh of her neck. Suki knew there was no hope for her.

Then, a brilliant white light exploded
in her eyes.

Voices shouted all around her. "Look!
It's the beast!"

The beast sprang away from Suki's limp body. The angry humans flashed their dazzling torches and edged closer to it.

In pain, Suki turned her head to see
the beast — it was Kendo, crouched in
a ring of torchlight. His fur had turned
grey and bristly. His eyes flamed red
with hatred. His face was pointy...
like a rat's.

But he was still her brother. Suki's
heart went out to him.

Suki saw the trap's teeth glinting
behind her brother, but she was too
weak to whisper a warning.

Kendo snarled at the humans and backed away. With a sickening crack, the jaws of the trap snapped shut.

For a second, the two cats' eyes met.
For a second, the brother Suki had
so dearly loved, returned and smiled
before his life faded away once again.

The Scaredy Cats stared at Kipling, their eyes as big as tennis balls. A voice called across the fields. "Fifi! Fifi!"

"Th-th-they're calling me home," Fifi said nervously. "Wh-wh-what happened to Suki and Professor Frankatstein?"

"They found the professor ranting in the street, claiming he had created life. They found a nice hospital for him, with strong bars on the windows. Suki went with him. She felt safe there – where nothing could come back to life and find her again . . . "

SCAREDY CATS

Shoo Rayner

☐ Frankatstein	1 84362 440 0	£8.99
☐ Foggy Moggy Inn	1 84362 441 9	£8.99
☐ Catula	1 84362 442 7	£8.99
☐ Catkin Farm	1 84362 443 5	£8.99
☐ Bluebeard's Cat	1 84362 444 3	£8.99
☐ The Killer Catflap	1 84362 445 1	£8.99
☐ Dr Catkyll and Mr Hyde	1 84362 446 X	£8.99
☐ Catnapped	1 84362 447 8	£8.99

Little HORRORS

☐ The Swamp Man	1 84121 646 1	£3.99
☐ The Pumpkin Man	1 84121 644 5	£3.99
☐ The Spider Man	1 84121 648 8	£3.99
☐ The Sand Man	1 84121 650 X	£3.99
☐ The Shadow Man	1 84362 021 X	£3.99
☐ The Bone Man	1 84362 010 3	£3.99
☐ The Snow Man	1 84362 009 X	£3.99
☐ The Bogey Man	1 84362 011 1	£3.99

These books are available from all good bookshops,
or can be ordered direct from the publisher:
Orchard Books, PO BOX 29, Douglas IM99 1BQ
Credit card orders please telephone 01624 836000 or fax 01624 837033
or e-mail: bookshop@enterprise.net for details.

To order please quote title, author and ISBN and your full name and address.
Cheques and postal orders should be made payable to 'Bookpost plc'.
Postage and packing is FREE within the UK
(overseas customers should add £1.00 per book).

Prices and availability are subject to change.